Under the Sea

ABCs

written and illustrated by

Liliana Gladysh

ISBN: 978-1-943201-24-2
Library of Congress Control Number: 2019933963

First Published by AM Ink Publishing LLC
www.AMInkPublishing.com

For my professor- Sandra Garvey

Thank you for sparking the love

of education and literature in me

Sea anemone are called the flower of the sea.

Anemone have no back bone.

Anemone come in

Beluga whales have a thick layer of blubber that keep them warm in icy cold water.

B is for beluga whale

Beluga's heart weighs 12 pounds.

The Great Barrier Reef is the biggest coral reef.

Coral reefs are made of tiny animals called "polyps."

C is for coral reef

Dolphins use a blowhole on top
of their head to breathe.

When dolphins are sick and hurt,

other dolphins come to help.

D is for dolphin

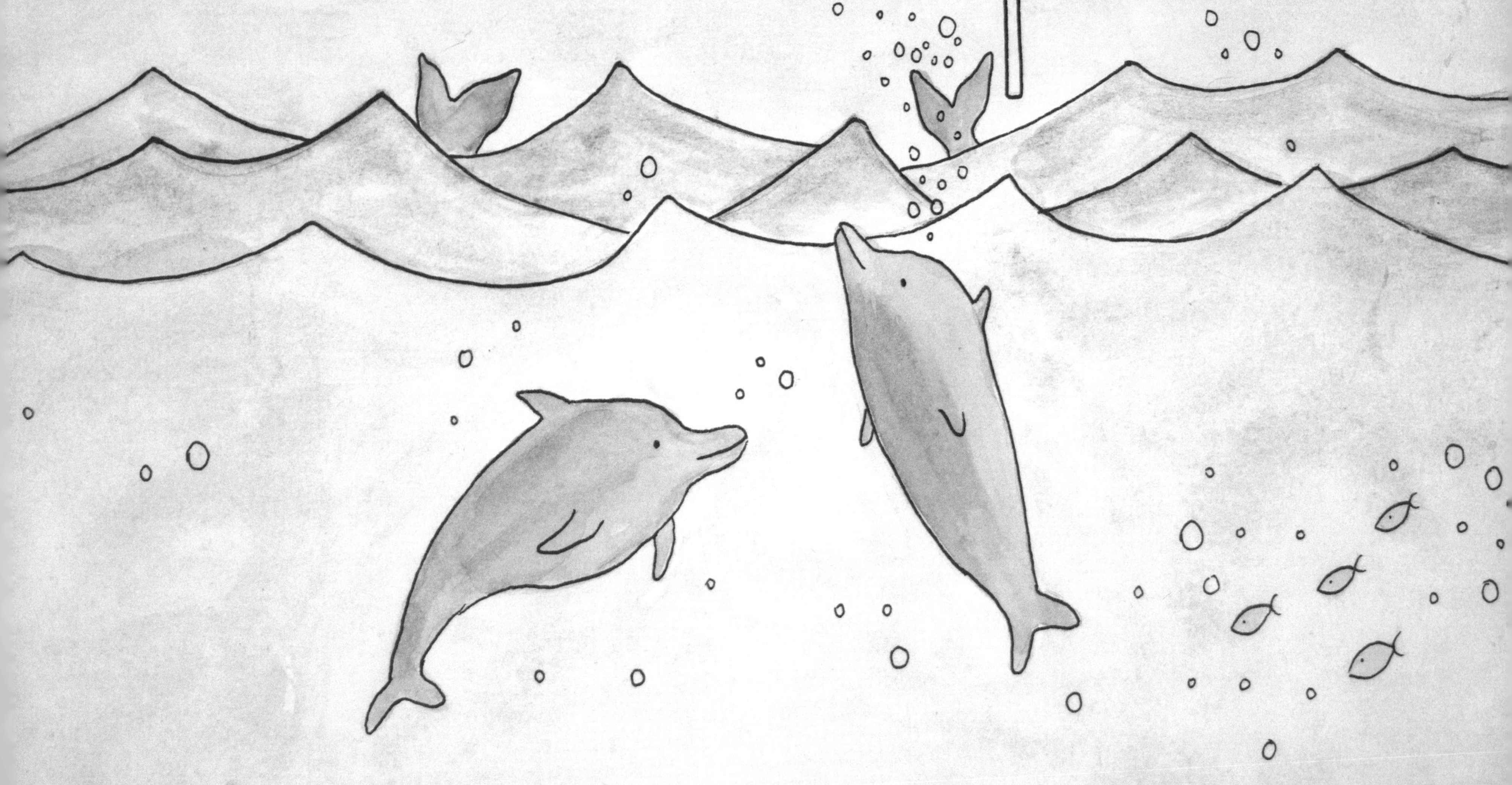

Elephant seals hunt for fish, squid, octopus and eel.

F is for flat fish

There are two types of flat fish:

soles and flounder.

Flounder hide in sand.

You can see baby guppies' eyes before they're even born.

No two guppies are alike!

G is for guppy

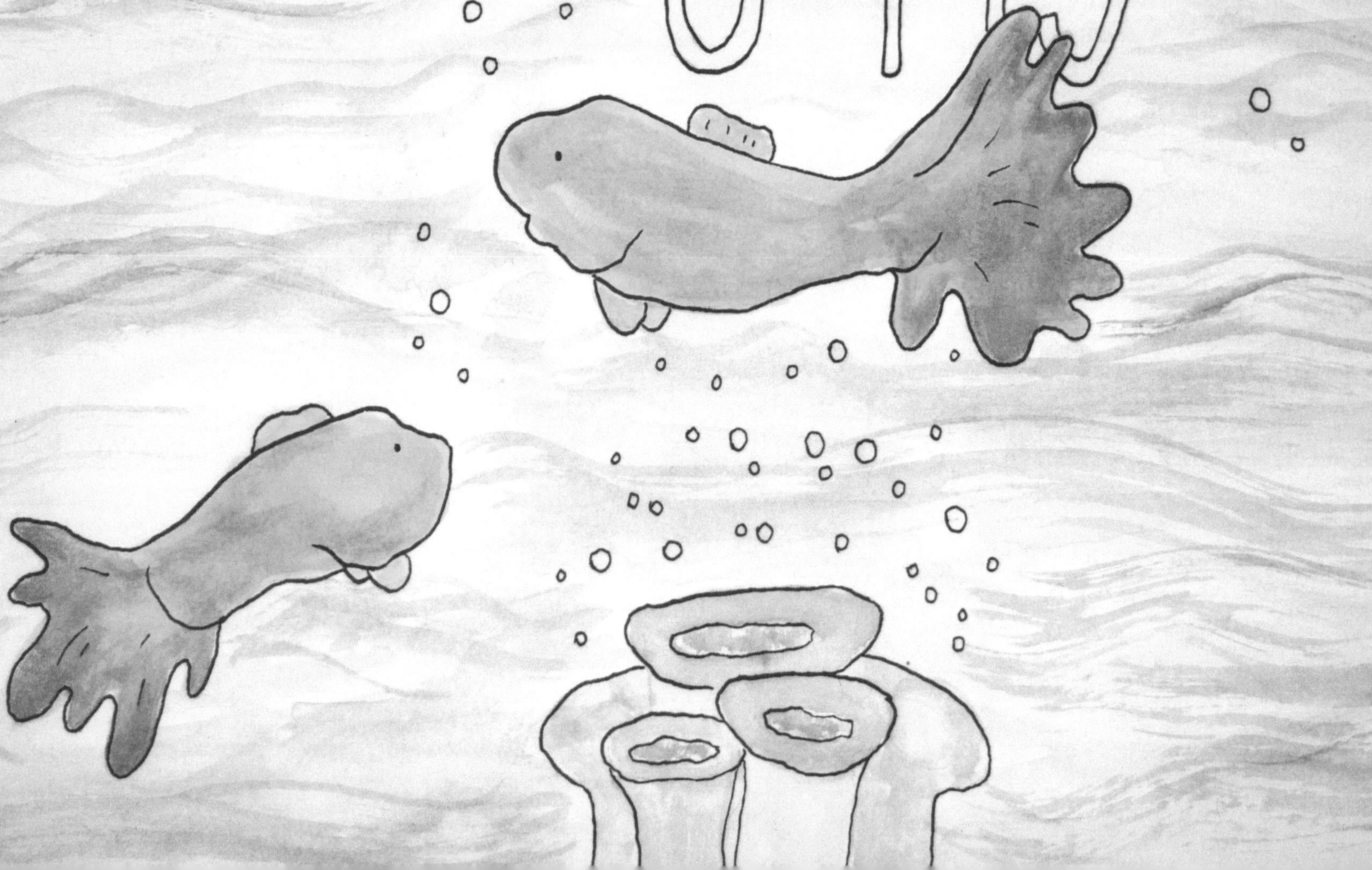

H is for humpback whale

Humpback whales can make sounds that are called "whale songs."

and horseshoe crab

Horseshoe crabs break their food using bristles on their legs.

I is for Indian

Indian glassfish live in fresh water.

Indian glassfish do not like to live alone.

Jellyfish look like umbrellas.

Jellyfish have no brains.

K is for

Kelp has many leaves called "blades."

kelp

Kelp live in cold waters.

L is for lionfish

Lionfish live in coral reefs.

Lionfish tentacles have stingers.

and lobster

Lobster eggs are called roe.

M is for minnows

Minnows are the largest of all fish families.

and mussels

You can find pearls in freshwater mussels.

N is for narwhal

Narwhals have black and white skin.

and nautilus

Nautilus can live more than 15 years in the wild.

Octopus have blue blood.

O is for octopus and

orca

Orca are also called "killer whales."

P is for

Puffer fish swallow water

So other fish can't swallow them.

puffer fish

Q is for Queen

Queen Angelfish eat sea sponges.

Angelfish

Queen Angelfish have blue lips.

R is for

S is for starfish

Starfish have eye spots on tips of their arms.

and seahorse

Seahorses are the fish that swim the slowest.

T is for turtle

Sometimes sea turtles cry to get rid of excess sea salt, not because they're sad.

The leatherback turtle can grow to be the size of a small boat.

U is for urchin

Urchins walk on tiny tube feet.

Urchins eat algae.

V is for velvet crab

Velvet crabs use back claws to swim.

Crabs are omnivores. They eat meat and plants.

X is for x-ray fish

Y is for yellow-tang fish

Yellow-tang fish live in coral reefs.

People like to keep them in fish tanks.

Z is for zebra

The stripes on a zebra shark change into spots when they grow older.

Zooplankton are tiny animals that swim in water.

shark

and zooplankton

ABOUT THE AUTHOR AND ILLUSTRATOR

Liliana Gladysh is a teacher, artist and lover of the oceanside. She grew up most of her life in Massachusetts. Liliana has a big heart for education and missions in which she plans to earn her degree in. Her inspiration to create comes from nature and travel adventures.

To learn more about Liliana's story, please visit her website at www.mayakcollections.com

CPSIA information can be obtained
at www.ICGtesting.com
Printed in the USA
LVRC081110120521
687203LV00003B/61